POISON & PORCHES

MRS. POMOLO INVESTIGATES

DONNA MUSE

Tica House
Publishing
Sweet Romance that Delights and Enchants!

CLICK HERE to Join our Reader's Club and to Receive Tica House Updates!

https://cozymystery.subscribemenow.com/

CONTENTS

[1]

It was late August. The first cool breeze of the season had just blown in, stirring the boughs of the aspens that lined the property like potatoes being whisked in a bowl. Geneva Pomolo had placed an empty soda carton on the front porch for one of the neighborhood cats, a ginger with black spots, who had instantly made his home in it. As the cat ran up the steps, Geneva could see him peering through one of the holes in the box with his baleful, solemn eyes, like little slits. When Geneva emerged from the house an hour later with a saucer of milk, she found the front porch newly carpeted with orange and red and brown leaves; the trees of the front yard were divesting themselves of their summer plumage.

Back inside, her housemate, Iris Reeves, was seated at the table by the kitchen window tinkering with a black boxy device that reminded Geneva of a ham radio. As Iris turned the knobs of the thing, a persistent snowy static gave way to the sound of muffled voices.

"They're talking," said Iris. "I can *almost* make out what they're talking about, but not quite."

"What do policemen talk about when they're not on a case?" said Geneva, lighting a scented rosemary candle and setting it down in the center of the table. "Probably nothing worth listening to."

Iris pulled another couple of grapes from the bowl sitting in front of her. She had been seated there for much of the afternoon wrangling with her new police scanner, which she had bought off a man at the Steamy Bean Café who said he specialized in appliances.

"What are the odds that salesman was lying, though?" murmured Iris. "He was so charming and persistent, I could hardly say no."

"What do we even need a police scanner for?" said Geneva, sitting down in the chair opposite. A cool wind whispered at the window. In the yard across the street, their neighbor with only four fingers on his right hand was gathering the first of the leaves in black trash bags. "If we want to know something, we can simply ask them."

"Haven't you noticed that Gerry has been sort of avoiding us lately?" asked Iris. "I think he's embarrassed that he keeps getting shown up by a couple of old ladies. I don't think he's ever bagged a single crook on his own. I bet they make fun of him down at the station."

"Homicide really isn't his beat," Geneva pointed out. She had just finished baking a challah bread, which she was now cutting into slices and slathering with butter from a grey plastic tub. "Just the other morning he stopped a robbery in progress at the convenience store on Fuller. Bullet went whizzing right past his ear. It could have killed him."

"That would be a loss," said Iris, a little distractedly. "I suppose his wife would miss him."

"You'd miss him, too, after a day or two," Geneva replied. Gerry was the only reason she and Iris were even tolerated by the Wrangler's Hill PD; he had lobbied for their assistance in investigating crimes in an amateur capacity when the rest of the station stood opposed. But his faith had been well-placed, for the two women had rewarded him by solving over a dozen cases.

With a groan of frustration, Iris brought her palm down, hard, on the scanner—so hard that Geneva nearly dropped the knife she was holding. A second later, the box crackled to life and a man's voice rang, clear and pristine, through the kitchen.

"I don't know what to tell ya. I'm probably the last person you should be asking about women."

"That's Lieutenant Sheehan," cried Iris in a triumphant tone.

"I've been married for almost ten years now," he went on, "and I don't pretend to understand my wife any better than the day I married her."

"Like I said," said Geneva. "Not particularly enlightening."

But then a second voice spoke, one that they both instantly recognized.

"Yeah, I hear you," said Gerry. "I wish I'd paid more attention during my Intro to Psych class, because her behavior lately has been completely baffling."

Iris raised an inquisitive brow at her partner.

"What's she been doing?" asked Lieutenant Sheehan.

They could almost hear Gerry squirming uncomfortably. "She keeps telling me she's going over to visit friends. But you know how you can almost smell it when your partner is lying? I started getting that vibe, so I phoned Veronica, and she hadn't seen her the whole night. Neither had Brittany or Jolene. Finally, last week I tailed her when she left the house —turns out she's been going line-dancing at a local country-western dance hall."

"She seeing anybody?" asked Sheehan.

"No, and that's what makes it so bizarre." There was a noise as though Gerry was thumping his hand on the dashboard of the car. "She was just dancing and having a good time. Didn't look like she was there to see anyone. If she's cheating on me, she's doing a good job of hiding it."

"You jealous?"

"I mean, a little," said Gerry. "But jealous of who? There's no one to be jealous of. I just wish she would tell me where she was really going—or, I don't know, invite me to go with her. Does she think I wouldn't love to go line-dancing?"

"Maybe she don't know any such thing," said Sheehan. "How long you two been married?"

"Round twenty-five years now."

"Maybe that's the problem. You spend enough time with someone, you assume you know everything about 'em. She probably didn't know you'd like to have been invited."

"Huh." There was a silence in which Gerry seemed to be considering this.

Iris shut off the scanner, looking a little guilty.

"Maybe we shouldn't have been listening to that," she said quietly.

Geneva shrugged as if to say, "Too late now." Aloud she said, "I wonder what's going on with Gerry and Kayla?"

"It sounds like she wanted to go dancing and got tired of waiting around to be invited," said Iris, who had a passion for dancing. "I wouldn't put up with that in a husband."

"You'd marry a swing-dancing champion," said Geneva. She placed one of the challah slices on a little plate and passed it over to Iris, who accepted it eagerly. "Anyway, the bigger question is why they're just 'chilling,' as the kids say, when they should be out finding whoever's been stealing the local dogs."

On a cool morning the week before, a woman had phoned the police station reporting that her dog had gone missing. She had let her Pomeranian out, and when she returned to fetch it a few minutes later, it had up and vanished. At the time, no one had taken her too seriously; the police figured the dog had probably run off and would come back.

But then a neighbor woman rang up the station saying she had seen a creature "sort of like a bear, with glowing red eyes" descend on the dog and carry her off in its mouth. This report made it into the local news, where it was widely spoofed. The next morning there were comics depicting the "Wrangler's Devil" in the *Beacon* funny pages—but then another dog disappeared, and then a cat, and then three chickens belonging to the Blaine family. Suddenly the prospect of a dangerous creature loose in Wrangler's didn't seem so absurd.

Gerry still wasn't buying it, though. "It's a classic example of myth-making," he told the girls when they pressed him about it. "We've had reports of hovering lights in the sky—that's all they were, lights—and three days later you've got people going on local access television saying they witnessed a space-ship with windows descend and three faceless humanoid figures step out. And they're not lying, they truly believe this happened. Myth-making can be very powerful."

"But a mass hallucination wouldn't have stolen a dozen animals," Iris pointed out.

Gerry glared, looking a little irritated. "Animals go missing in this town every week. Normally, nobody notices because there's not some absurd story about a hyena or whatever connected to it. If anything, we owe Mrs. Briars a favor for drawing the public's attention to a problem in this town—" and here he launched into a long lecture on the responsibility of homeowners to guard their animals and keep them from running rampant. Neither Geneva nor Iris came away convinced.

"I suppose we're lucky that no one has been killed yet," said Iris, placing a slice of Brie cheese between two crackers. "It's only a matter of time before somebody is mauled by Gerry's mass delusion."

"You think he'll ever listen to us?" said Geneva, gazing through the window at the box where the cat knelt, vigilant and sly. A familiar-looking beat-up sedan came shambling down the street and came to a slow stop on the curb at the front of the house. "That's the nice thing about George—if anything, he's too attentive."

George Wilson was Geneva's gentleman friend, a timid and gentle poet who at present was walking up the drive in a rumpled grey suit and a battered-looking fedora. Just before reaching the door, he knelt and attempted to pat the ginger cat, but the cat hissed and shot its paw out of the box. George winced, looking betrayed.

Geneva rose to greet him with a kiss on the cheek as he stepped into the living room. "You doing all right, dear?" she asked.

George shook his head with a crestfallen air. "What is that line in Shakespeare? 'True is it that we have seen better days.'"

Geneva shot a worried glance at Iris. George typically resorted to poetry when he was feeling so burdened that he couldn't find his own words. "Do you want to talk about it?"

George kicked off his shoes in front of the door and sank down into the sofa, looking as though he wanted it to swallow him up.

"You want anything to drink?" asked Iris.

"Lemon water, if you don't mind."

Iris bustled toward the fridge for the filtered water pitcher. Geneva seated herself in the rocking chair opposite the sofa, smiling patiently.

"Some men," said George in a voice crackling with annoyance, "are just—" and here he uttered a string of words clearly displaying his angst and frustration.

"George!" said Geneva in a tone of surprise. "What's happened?"

Iris came hurrying into the living room carrying a tall glass of water, all eagerness. "Yes, do tell," she said. "I want to hear every sordid detail."

George shuddered a little, although it was not cold in the room.

"Every Tuesday night," he said, "I go out with some guys from church. You already know that. There's that club in the West End that has open mic nights, and people get up there and play music and read poetry and do comedy routines. It's a great way for up-and-coming musicians in Wrangler's Hill to get noticed. I heard of a woman who got a record deal because she happened to be performing on a night when a talent scout was seated in the audience.

"Well, anyway, last Tuesday I'd had one too many beers, and I decided I'd go up there and read some of my poetry—"

"Oh, George!" cried Geneva, hands over her mouth. "That was... well, that was very brave of you."

"Brave, nothing," said George. "I was a bit tipsy and not thinking too straight. I got up there and read a couple poems —one about the vastness of space and the other about you, Gen. The applause was warm, and the audience really seemed to have liked it. But when I returned to my seat the guys were just awful about it."

"What did they say?" asked Iris.

"Terrible things," said George. "Some of which I won't bother to repeat. They said I should quit with the poetry, that writing is for weenies, one of them kept calling me a 'simp'— I'm not even sure what that is. The thing that really got me, though, was that they kept saying you and I weren't really dating."

"What do you mean?" said Geneva. "Of course, we're dating."

"I tried to tell them that." George shifted miserably. "But they weren't having it. They said it didn't make sense that an old soppy poet like me could be in a relationship. They said women don't want to date wannabe poets, and that I probably made it all up." George's face burned a little as he recalled the discussion. "Gen, I got the impression they didn't think you really exist."

"Of course, they know I exist," said Geneva. "They've seen us together at church, haven't they?"

"They said you were probably my sister."

"They're just giving you a hard time. They know perfectly well I exist and that I'm not your sister. I wouldn't pay them any mind."

This did little to console George, however. "I enjoy going to the club," he said. "It's one of the few times I get a chance to go and hang out with other guys. How am I going to show my face there again if they keep ribbing me like that?"

"Well, I would suggest finding better friends," said Geneva. "But if you really want to show them up, I can come with you next week. I don't have anything planned that night, and I bet any one of those guys wish they had a steady date."

"They're just jealous, honestly," said Iris, setting down another glass of lemon water (for George had drunk his first in a single fluid gulp). "None of them are in loving relationships that I know of. I know that group of men. They're baffled that you won Geneva, who is probably the best catch in town."

Geneva blushed behind her wire-frame spectacles.

"Well, I'll do my best to make them jealous when I show up on your arm Tuesday night," she said. "I'm going to wear my prettiest gown—maybe get my hair styled—maybe buy some new shoes—and then let them *try* to say I'm not a real person! *Or* your sister."

[2]

In the four days that followed this conversation in Iris's living room, several things happened.

First, a goat belonging to a farmer on the outskirts of Wrangler's Hill was found dead in a dense wood about a mile from the farm, claw marks across its neck and chest. Already conspiracies were percolating online about men in flying saucers picking up farm animals and transporting them across town.

The police, however, had settled on a more mundane explanation. They were sure that the goat theft and the recent disappearances of pets were the work of local delinquents, ranging in age from seventeen to twenty, who were trying to stoke panic.

"Presumably these are well-fed young men," said Lieutenant Sheehan, "so thieving for poverty is out of the question. We're not talking Jean Valjean here."

But this explanation failed to satisfy reporters for the *Beacon* and the various news affiliates, who wanted to know what would provoke a teenage boy to drag a goat's body a full mile through the woods and then unceremoniously dump it in a clearing. Lieutenant Sheehan looked flustered. Watching the press conference on television, Geneva couldn't say whether he was deliberately trying to mislead the press to avoid panic or he had really convinced himself that "local boys" were the source of all the trouble because the alternative was too mysterious to contemplate. Iris, sipping a raspberry tea as she peddled her exercise bike, snorted in derision.

"Boys, right," she said, and the corners of her mouth twitched. "How big do you think this creature is, and why hasn't animal control been called out yet?"

"I don't know if Wrangler's Hill animal control is equipped to deal with this sort of deadly creature," said Geneva. "Probably easier for the police to just deny, deny, deny, and hope whatever it is goes away during the winter."

"Fat chance of that happening," said Iris, peddling all the harder. "You'll notice it's lifting bigger and bigger animals each week. I bet this thing is growing. Pretty soon, it'll be unbolting doors and marching into people's houses."

"Maybe we should leave out a leg of mutton or something on the front porch," Geneva replied drily.

"Mutton, land's sake! It'll be wanting the keys to the place."

The next thing that happened was that Geneva phoned Gerry and, in the process of grilling him about the mysterious creature (he repeated the company line about delinquents, though he clearly didn't believe it), invited him and Kayla to go out with them on Tuesday night. Gerry texted back a few hours later to say that he had raised the suggestion to Kayla, who had politely declined.

"Said she's already made plans for that night," Gerry said. "Gen, I'm sorry about that."

Geneva pondered this as she was getting ready late Tuesday afternoon. She had known Gerry and Kayla for some time now, and Kayla had never seemed anything less than devoted to her husband, but Geneva supposed even the most loving spouses needed a break from their partners now and again. She worried more for Gerry, who didn't seem to understand this and was taking it badly. Last Sunday morning, she and Iris had driven past the Spiced Brandy Coffeetorium and found him standing in the parking lot, gazing out at a field full of shrubs and bracken, sporting a three-day growth of beard and a haunted look.

"I guess I'm lucky, in a way, that George has always been so good to me," she said as she inserted her elephant earrings. Iris stood at a vanity in the adjoining room swathed in a fog of perfume. "I was reluctant to go out with him at first—I didn't think I would date anyone ever again after Arthur died—but he's been good to me."

"You should *marry* him," cried Iris, who never passed up an opportunity to lobby for Geneva and George to be married.

Geneva ignored this. "I should tell him I love him more often. He could be sliced to pieces by the Wrangler's Hill Devil on one of his jogs around the neighborhood, and I'd spend the rest of my life wishing I had been more expressive."

"Has it occurred to anyone that maybe we're dealing with a werewolf?" asked Iris. "I'm surprised a full-scale search hasn't been mounted yet."

"As long as the 'werewolf' is only stealing animals, I don't think the police are going to search too hard for it," Geneva replied.

George showed up at the house at around seven to pick them both up. He was wearing his usual rumpled charcoal suit and battered hat with a necktie that was too long for him. Geneva thought he looked a bit like Leonard Cohen if Leonard Cohen had been a down-on-his-luck Bohemian Midwestern poet.

"You look lovely, dear," she said as she kissed him on the cheek near the entrance to the kitchen.

"I'm still not sure this is a smart move," said George, hands jammed in his coat pockets. "You could be Marilyn Monroe and they'd find a way to make fun of me."

"Do I not look like Marilyn Monroe?" said Geneva in a tone of feigned disappointment.

"You look prettier than Marilyn Monroe," George replied. "That's not the point. I feel as though I'm doing you a disservice, dragging you to this club where these guys are just going to roast me. Or you. Or both of us."

"George, dear, surely you're exaggerating. Besides, I'm not doing this for myself." Geneva tugged at his tie playfully. "I'm happy to go with you and make a statement. We *are* dating."

"Anyway," said Iris, pouring herself a glass of orange juice at the kitchen counter, "why do you even want to impress these guys? Why do you continue to spend time with them if they're such dweebs?"

George looked as though he hadn't considered this. "If I severed ties, I would... Well, I don't know."

"Sweetie, we could always find a new church if it will make you more comfortable." Geneva removed his hat and adjusted it so that it looked less battered. "Maybe next week, we'll figure out where Kayla is really going on her nights out and invite ourselves to join her. Wouldn't that be fun?"

"So fun," George said in a doubtful tone.

Iris set down her glass on the counter with a loud clunk. "Everyone got your weapons at the ready?"

"Weapons?" repeated Geneva.

Iris nodded serenely and held up a switchblade with a glinting handle. "You'd be a fool to go anywhere in this town right now without being armed. I bought pepper spray for the both of you—" and reaching into her purse she began pulling out small bottles of pepper spray which she handed to both of them.

Geneva stared down at hers with a bemused look. "Iris, dear, how is pepper spray going to protect me from a werewolf?"

"You'll need to hit him right between the eyes," said Iris, "so aim carefully."

It was a mark of how grave the situation had gotten in the past week that no one much objected to this. Placing the spray in her purse, Geneva opened the door and stepped out onto the front porch, where a blast of cool night air hit her. Somewhere in the boughs of the tallest aspen, an owl was hooting as if to say hello. George knelt down to scratch the neighbor-hood cat—who surprisingly didn't resist him this time—while they waited for Iris to finish locking the door.

"You know, we really ought to give him a name," said Geneva, as the cat purred contentedly and nuzzled George's hand.

"I like the name Pierre," said George, who had finally succumbed to Geneva's entreaties and begun reading *War and Peace*. "Because he goes from house to house and lets other people feed him, is beloved of the whole village, although he contributes nothing—"

"'His purse is always empty 'cause it's open to all,'" sang Iris, quoting the words of the song as she led them off the porch and down into the drive. She motioned to the moon, which had reached its zenith and stood looming over the trees like a great wheel of Brie. "Well, if we were ever going to meet a werewolf, I suppose tonight would be the night."

The Seven Swine was already beginning to fill by the time they arrived. It took the little group of three several minutes to make their way through a wood-paneled atrium into the dimly lit lounge where men and women sat together at circular tables draped in crisp white linen, sipping rum and martinis and speaking in low whispers to an exhausted-looking waitstaff.

A pinched-looking woman of around nineteen stood at the mic and did a breathy comedic routine about the rigors of college life and the hassles of continuing to live with her parents which drew tepid applause. As Geneva, George and Iris were being seated, she left the stage, rather in a hurry, and a young man galloped onstage after her to a hip-hop beat, motioning for the audience to clap along.

Iris leaned over to George and said in an exaggerated whisper, "Hey, now it looks like you're dating two women. All the better." And she laughed.

A woman seated at a table in front of them, wearing a long white evening gown and cooling herself with a fan (for the intense concentration of bodies in such a small space had indeed raised the temperature in the room considerably), let out a disdainful sniff. "This is *not* what we came here to see," she said in a voice that carried. "If you would kindly escort the gentleman off the stage..."

She spoke in a voice of such conviction that Geneva glanced around, half-expecting a member of staff to march up and escort the young man to the door. No one else seemed to be paying her any attention, however, and the lack of attention seemed to annoy her even more than the hip-hop.

She leaned over in the direction of a woman seated next to her, a woman in a simple rose-colored smock who wore in her hair a matching hair-clip and was watching the stage with a look of studied concentration. From the posture of the two women toward each other, Geneva deduced that they were old friends.

"I suppose they just let *anyone* make music these days," said the woman in the gown who was the older of the two by some years.

"Maribel, I would never presume to contradict you," said the second woman, though she plainly wanted to do so, "but some people really like this music. It's far more popular than rock n' roll."

The woman named Maribel rolled her eyes theatrically. "No one *I* know listens to it," she said, though Geneva doubted she had any friends under sixty. "Is this the sort of music millennials listen to as they sit at home in their parents' basements? No wonder they can't find employment."

"This woman seems like a barrel of laughs," muttered Iris, who had given up trying to listen to the performance.

Maribel turned to her left, where sat a young woman tuning a guitar with an unhappy look. She wore a flannel shirt, jeans that were fashionably ripped at the knees, and a black choker. She had dyed her hair in neon pink strips that alternated with her natural auburn. On the fingers of her right hand were long, lethal-looking chrome nails that put Geneva in mind of

Wolverine's claws. She seemed to be making an active effort not to listen or engage with the loud-mouthed older woman seated at the table next to her.

But Maribel didn't seem to notice, for she said in a hectoring tone, leaning toward the woman in the jeans, "Leora, is this the sort of music you play? Don't tell me you're planning to go up there and perform this garbage."

"No, Maribel," said Leora slowly, through gritted teeth. "I told you, I'm not a hip-hop artist, I'm a folk singer."

"I don't care what you call it," said Maribel, leaning back and stirring her martini with a languid air, "all music today sounds the same to me. Indie, folk, rap, it's all vile. If you can't sing it in front of your grandmother, why even bother putting it on an album?" As if looking for affirmation, she cast around for the nearest available older person and settled on Geneva. "You wouldn't listen to this if they paid you, would you?"

"We're listening to it now," Iris butted in.

Maribel scowled. "Yes, but you couldn't have known this is what they would be playing when you came in. I've half a mind to lodge a formal complaint with the manager of this joint."

And, to the horror of the two women seated on either side of her, who both visibly flinched, Maribel held up a hand and said, "Waiter, would you tell me how I can get hold of the manager? I have some issues with tonight's entertainment."

The waiter in question, a young black man who was clearly disgusted, said curtly, "Contact information is available on our website."

[3]

GENEVA HAD CEASED PAYING attention to the rapper, she was now so thoroughly engrossed in the drama playing out in the seats in front of her. She wondered what relationship these three women bore to each other. The girl named Leora (she seemed only a girl to Geneva, though she must have been at least twenty-five) clearly couldn't wait to ascend the stage and get away from the woman seated beside her. A faint, indefinable air of guilt hung over her, as though she half-regretted the career she had chosen, yet she was still determined that it was the only field in which she was capable of doing anything memorable.

"Well, thank God that's over," said Maribel over the resounding applause that accompanied the completion of the rapper's song. "Maybe the worst is over." Then, seeing that

Leora was preparing to take the stage, she quickly added, "Oh, perhaps not."

Leora shot her a resentful glare that transformed with remarkable speed into a smile as she stepped in front of the mic. Slowly she began strumming the guitar.

"How are you all doing tonight?" She spoke in a low, husky voice, and the crowd murmured replies. "My name is Leora Kismet. I've released one album independently. I'm not yet signed to a label, but I'm working on it. Sorry I don't have the full band with me tonight, they couldn't all make it." She smiled hopefully. "Maybe next week."

"Stop apologizing and get on with it!" groused Maribel. "This is taking forever."

This outburst proved too much for the staff. The waiter approached her again and said quietly, so as not to cause even more disruption, "Ma'am, if you keep interrupting, I'm going to have to ask you to leave."

Maribel glared at him resentfully, as if to say she had the right to holler out whatever and whenever she wanted. "Last I heard this was a free country," she said. "Nobody orders me around."

"Rules of the establishment, ma'am," the waiter replied. "We have the right to refuse service to any customer. Surely, you don't want to be embarrassed in front of these people."

"The only person you're embarrassing is yourself," Maribel shot back.

Ignoring the tiff going on below, and the fact that half the room had now turned to face the old woman, Leora launched into her song. It was a stirring and melancholy ballad about a girl in a red cap and scarf stumbling home through a snowstorm, not sure if she was going to make it home or not. As Leora sang, she tried to look everywhere but at the scene unfolding in front of her.

"Maribel, *really*," said the woman seated next to her, facing the stage. "Some of us are trying to enjoy the performance."

"You can put a lid on it, Janna," said Maribel waspishly. "Nobody asked you."

Janna flexed her knotted hands. "I've been in your employ for nearly twenty years," she said. "The least you could do is listen to me once in a while."

"As soon as you say something worth saying," said Maribel, "I will."

Not seeing any way of cordially replying to this, Janna redirected her attention to the stage. Leora was nearing the climax of the song; the little girl in the red scarf was just a few hundred yards from home, but she had fallen into one of the snowdrifts and now the ghost of her dead grandmother was descending to escort her to heaven. Iris sniffed audibly; a few of the women around them were crying. Maribel rolled her eyes in annoyance.

"Whatever happened to Hendrix?" she said. "The Rolling Stones? Led Zeppelin? They were real musicians and *men*, not like this inane garbage we've got now."

"Funny, I remember my mother saying the same thing in the sixties," murmured Janna.

"Excuse me?"

"Nothing," said Janna sweetly.

From the tone in her voice, Geneva sensed that Janna wasn't a great admirer of her employer. She wondered what had compelled her to stay twenty years in the service of someone she clearly disliked. Maybe Maribel hadn't always been like this. Some people got notably crabbier in their old age, as their faculties declined.

Leora, meanwhile, was faltering, her voice breaking up slightly as the song reached its conclusion. Tears filled her eyes as she scrambled to finish the song before she broke down entirely.

"Truly weak," interjected Maribel.

As Leora's playing slowed, she rose from the stool on which she had been sitting. "Sorry, I was going to play two or three more songs, but... like I said, I'm really sorry."

Taking her guitar, she ran offstage before the audience had even begun clapping.

Iris, never one to shy away from confrontation, immediately rounded on the old woman. "Honestly," she said, "we might have gotten a full set if you hadn't been running your awful mouth the entire time."

"Well! I *never*." Maribel bawled her hands into little fists and made an exaggerated motion of rubbing tears out of her eyes. "If you liked that miserable cornball song so much you could just buy her album. No one else did."

Geneva thought she had never seen a woman so nakedly hostile to someone who hadn't done anything to her.

"Is that woman a friend of yours?" she asked, her voice purposefully non-conflictive. "Because that's a really sad way for you to treat a friend who wanted your support."

"She didn't invite me here for support," snapped Maribel, actually taking out a cigarette and lighting it. Blowing the smoke out of her mouth, she added, "She wanted my validation."

Geneva and Iris exchanged glances. They were both at a loss. Neither one knew how to curtail someone who positively refused to be shamed. "A three-year-old knows how to treat people better than this," muttered Iris.

"I'm sorry, are you lecturing me?" asked Maribel, punctuating the air with the lit cigarette. "Because I'll sue!"

"You can't sue someone for reprimanding you," said Iris, aghast.

"I'll sue you for being a public nuisance," Maribel shot back.

Iris was outraged, but she refused to be goaded further into such a ridiculous conversation.

The waiter came striding back over from the back of the room. Geneva thought he was really going to lead Maribel out of the room this time, but to her surprise he turned to them and said, "I'm sorry, ladies, but if the two of you are going to carry on like this, I'll need you to take it outside."

Suddenly, Geneva became painfully conscious that most of the rest of the room was looking, not at Maribel, but at her and Iris.

One of the men seated close to George, who had been watching the two women with a smirking expression, said, "George, would you kindly tell your women to calm down?"

"His women?" said a man in a black homburg. "One of them looks old enough to be his mom."

Several people laughed, including Maribel, while George sank down into his seat with a grim face.

"I am sorry, sir," said Geneva, addressing herself to the waiter. "All we did was politely ask this woman to stop heckling the performers—"

"I've already discussed that with her," said the beleaguered waiter. "And don't you worry, she's going out next."

But Maribel sat back and took a swig of her martini, plainly enjoying herself. It was clear she didn't believe the waiter would do a thing to her. "Now *this* is the sort of entertainment I paid for," she said to him. "Keep it up!"

But by now, no one was paying her much mind. The focus had definitely shifted to Geneva and her party.

"Again, I'm sorry," said Geneva. "We were trying to defend that performer who cut her set short so she could run to the back and cry. In truth, I feel downright sorry for her."

"That 'performer' was with me," said Maribel, sitting up straighter. "We came together."

"That only makes it worse," said Geneva sadly.

It was at this point that a bulky security guard in a grey uniform, wearing an earpiece in one ear, appeared at Geneva's elbow. Bending closer, he said, "We've had report of a disturbance over here? If you could just see your way to the exit—"

Geneva turned a pleading look at George, who was watching the debacle with a helpless expression. Seeing his one chance at valor slipping away, and perhaps emboldened by the derisive snickers of his church-going companions, George stood up behind the security guard, as if wanting to overpower him, which of course, was ludicrous.

"You need to leave her be," he announced in his roughest voice.

"George, no," cried Geneva.

But the threat had already been made, and the damage had already been done. No sooner had she warned George, than a second security guard came creeping up behind George and, with a single well-placed grasp on his arm, took him dragging toward the exit. Geneva and Iris followed quickly behind until the door was shut in their faces, and she and George and Iris stood on the cold sidewalk.

[4]

"Well, that maybe could have gone better," said Geneva.

They were heading home down the mostly deserted streets of central Wrangler's Hill, George in the back seat still mumbling about a hurt arm. Iris's glasses were askew, and the sleeve of her floral party dress had been marred in the scuffle. Geneva had just received a text from the club informing her that neither she nor her friends were welcome back in the club ever again. Geneva regretted having given her phone number to the hostess earlier to be entered into a drawing for a prize of four free meals.

"Are they allowed to do that?" asked Iris. "Forbid you from returning?"

"They can do whatever they want," said Geneva. "They're a private establishment. Still, you'd think they'd have done a better job of policing the real hecklers."

"Did you see what that old lady was wearing, though?" said Iris. "She looked like she was pretending to be royalty. I imagine she was thrown out next. I wish I could have seen her face when she was given the boot."

Geneva agreed. Still, the injustice rankled. They should have been left to enjoy the show, and Maribel should have been tossed out. Or at the very least, she should have been tossed out first.

Geneva turned and gave George a long, loving look. He had fallen asleep, using his fedora as a thin pillow against the window. "Poor George," she said, "he'll never be able to show his face in front of his rotten friends again."

"Honestly that might be for the best," said Iris, turning into their suburb. "Presumably he's also banned from the lounge after trying to overcome that security guard ... probably wouldn't hurt him to make some new friends."

"The way those guys were talking about us, that was what set me off." Geneva straightened the folds of her dress. "I probably wouldn't have gotten so involved if they hadn't been there. And that poor woman, Leonora..."

"Leora," said Iris.

"I'd like to get hold of her and invite her out for coffee and apologize for the way that woman was treating her. There are certain people who think they're entitled to lord it over everyone else around and treat other people as their personal footstools. When I saw how Maribel was treating her and the waiter, something inside me snapped. Poor girl wouldn't even stand up for herself, so I had to."

Seeing that she was still flustered, Iris turned on the radio to seek some soft, calming classical music. Instead, a symphony by Gustav Mahler began playing so loudly it rattled the windows, awakening George.

"What's happened?" he asked groggily. "Is that the last trump?"

"No, not even close to the last," said Geneva.

"I took the wheel because you were exhausted," said Iris. "You don't mind me driving, do you?"

George blinked slowly; he only just seemed to have realized he was riding in the back of his own car. "No, no, not at all," he said. "I didn't even hurt that guy, did I?"

Geneva turned to him with a benevolent smile. "You were simply terrifying, Georgie," she said sweetly. "Try not to worry yourself too much; we'll be home in a few minutes."

Before they retired to bed for the night, Geneva expressed a hope that things would begin to calm down a little. But the following day brought a string of bad news, one miserable item after another.

On the following evening after Iris returned home from work, Geneva borrowed her car to buy groceries. When she returned home at around six, she found Iris seated in the kitchen eating a cup of vanilla yogurt and listening to the police scanner with a perturbed look.

"I don't know if you heard," she said, "but I think the Wrangler's Devil may have just made his first kill."

Geneva half-wondered if she would ever be greeted with good news. Setting a carton of ice cream down on the counter, she asked, "Who died?"

"You won't believe this," said Iris, "but it's the woman we met last night at the club. The one who basically had us thrown out for disturbing the peace."

Such was Geneva's surprise that she forgot all about the bags still waiting in the half-open trunk. "You mean Maribel got killed by a wild animal only a day after a very public disturbance?"

Iris nodded. "I don't want to say it's convenient, but..."

"The timing is certainly odd," said Geneva. "Who's on the case?"

"Gerry and Sheehan." She turned a knob on the scanner. "Listen."

Geneva listened. Gerry was speaking; he sounded plainly flummoxed.

"I won't mince words," he said, "this looks bad. We've been ignoring this thing for upwards of three weeks, and now it goes and kills an old lady. If the media gets hold of this, we'll be run out of town."

"Do we know for sure it was a critter?" asked Sheehan.

"I mean, we won't *know*, know, until Quipling has finished looking over the body." Sarah Quipling was Wrangler Hill's resident coroner, the latest in a long line. "But there are claw marks all up and down her face and neck. Poor woman seems to have been mauled to death."

"I don't know if I would say 'poor woman,'" said Sheehan. "By all accounts, the woman seems to have been a terror."

"Even terrors don't deserve to be mauled." There was a distinct note of regret, mixed with pity, in Gerry's voice. "She may have been a nuisance to everyone she met, but I wouldn't wish that sort of death on anyone."

"Dear Gerry," said Iris, beaming.

"You reckon we ought to tell the girls?" said Sheehan.

There was a pause in which Gerry seemed to be considering the question. "I wouldn't worry about it; they'll be here soon enough. Sometimes I could swear they can sniff blood from ten miles off."

He probably hadn't meant it as a compliment, but Geneva smiled, nonetheless. "You want to wait until after dinner or do you think we ought to head over there now?"

"I don't know about you, but I completely lost my appetite, thinking of the creature clawing at that woman's face." Iris tossed her yogurt container into the waste bin. "I'd like to examine the crime scene before news of the killing starts getting around."

"I'll text Gerry and ask him for the address," said Geneva. "We'll finish getting the bags out of the car, and then we can go."

"I reckon you'd better hurry," said Iris, gazing through the bay window. "Looks like someone is already helping himself."

Geneva looked. Out in the driveway, a raccoon stood on its hind legs in the trunk, rifling through the bags with delicate, deft fingers. It had already pulled out a whole bag of mandarin orange chicken and tossed it aside into the grass, as if not finding it to its linking. Now it was attempting to open a two-liter bottle of cherry limeade.

Grabbing a broom from the pantry, Geneva ran to the door and flung it open. "Hey! You best get out of here before I get ahold of you!"

Badly startled, the raccoon hastily grabbed a bag of jalapeño bagels and scampered off.

"Animal control has really been slacking lately," said Iris, having followed Geneva. "This town is overrun with wild critters and now people are literally dying."

"You'd think we were pioneers living on the edge of the frontier," said Geneva, "not twenty-first century women in the suburbs having to protect their food from adventurous critters."

"It's enough to make one think about buying a pellet gun," said Iris, running back and grabbing her keys from the table. "I'll help you bring what's left of our food in, and we'll go."

[5]

THEY REACHED the house at about 6:45 that evening to find
Gerry and Sheehan standing forlornly on the front porch. It
was an old-fashioned wood-framed house painted in gaudy
pastel colors, roseate pink and robin's egg blue, looking much
as it must have looked when it was first built half a century or
more ago. A rose-patterned porch swing had been conspicu-
ously torn in places and bits of down had been ripped out of
it, the dull colors enlivened here and there with splashes of a
dark liquid. The sight of it set Geneva's stomach churning.

Gerry didn't even bother to ask how the two women had
learned of the murder. "Coroner's initial estimate is that she
must have died between four and five. She's still examining
the body but there's no doubt that she was killed by something large and powerful... a creature of some sort."

"Any guesses as to what sort of creature?" asked Iris.

"Unless there's a colony, I'd imagine we're dealing with the same creature in all these different reports," said Gerry. "Stolen chickens, mutilated goats, now an old woman… We could be dealing with anything from an alligator to a hyena."

"Or a wolf," said Iris, who hadn't given up hope.

Gerry shrugged, as if to concede the point. "There's not a lot of mystery to *how* this poor woman died. The real question is going to be how do we find this thing? How do we catch it?"

"It would help if anyone," said Sheehan irritably, "*anyone* had witnessed the attack, or had seen anything out of the ordinary."

"Have you tried canvassing the neighborhood?" asked Geneva. Dusk was falling, the air was cooling, and in houses all up and down the street she could see the faint blue light of televisions beaming from behind curtained windows. "I'd be happy to ask around."

"We spoke to a couple boys who had just returned home from soccer practice," said Gerry. "They hadn't seen anything. Woman a few houses down claims she left a pie cooling on her windowsill and it's gone, she really wanted us to look into it. She swears the creature stole it."

"Do you think it did?"

Gerry looked irritated by the question. "I told her we'd look into it."

Geneva guessed by the tone of his voice that he wasn't particularly fussed about a missing pie. He looked thoroughly irritated, as if blaming himself for the woman's death. "I don't know if this helps," she said, "but we had a run-in with this lady only last night."

Gerry glanced up in surprise. "Did you really? Of course, you did."

And together they told him about their trip to the Seven Swine, how Maribel had heckled seemingly every performer, and how they had ultimately been dragged from the room in front of everyone when they attempted to stand up to her.

"It certainly sounds as though she had some enemies," said Gerry, kicking at a loose acorn that had fallen from one of the several towering oaks in the front yard. "If this were a more traditional murder case, I should say we ought to start interviewing suspects, identifying who hated her most."

"Honestly, if the Devil hadn't killed her," said Iris, "someone else would have."

"I'd like to speak with both of those women," said Gerry. "Janna and the other one. We've searched the house, and it's currently empty, but it looks as though someone else lives here. We were sort of hoping they might turn up while we were waiting."

Not wanting to stay idle, Geneva said she was going to go knock on doors and Iris volunteered to come with her. In the house on their left, a woman in a tartan apron was presumably cooking dinner while behind her two children, aged about five and seven, watched *The Angry Beavers*.

"I'm sorry," she said, "I've already got a church," and began to close the door in their faces.

"Wait, we're not from a church," cried Geneva. "A woman has just been killed."

The woman froze in the act of closing the door, glanced behind her, and then stepped out onto the front step. She drew a cigarette from her dress pocket and lit it.

"What's all this about?"

"The woman who lived next door," said Iris. "Maribel, uh, I don't even know her last name. She was clawed to death by a creature, and we were wondering if you had seen anything."

"I'm sorry," she said, not looking particularly sorry. "I don't go over there. I tell my kids not to go over there. A *creature,* you say?"

"So I'm guessing you knew Maribel?" said Geneva.

"Unfortunately, yes. Every day I'll come out to water the plants, and she'll be sitting there on the front porch, mad about something or other. Never had a nice word to say. 'Hayley, do you ever regret getting knocked up at the age of nineteen?' she asked me once. 'Hayley, do you think those two boys will grow up to be idiots like their fathers?'" Hayley shrugged. "I'm not saying my kids are the brightest, but no mother likes to hear her kids run down like that."

"No, indeed."

Hayley frowned in a studied way, as if trying to conceal some secret joy. Up in the darkening skies, a single bird wheeled round in lazy circles.

"I know I'm supposed to love my neighbor, and pray for my enemy," she said, "and I'm sorry. I know this makes me a bad person, but I can't, I just can't. You can judge me all you like, but you didn't know this woman."

"We did, actually. Barely," said Geneva, and explained again how they had met on the previous night. "Anyway... maybe keep your kids indoors for a few days, until we learn more."

Haley glanced solemnly round as if expecting the Wrangler's Devil to be lurking behind the herbaceous border. "Do you really think it could come back? Do you think it might hurt Darryl or Evan?"

"Ma'am, it might have killed a grown woman in her seventies," said Iris. "There's no telling what it could do."

They turned and made the walk back up the drive, but Hayley remained in the door for a moment or two watching with a wary expression. "Looks like the funeral won't be too crowded," said Iris. "We might be the only ones there."

"Oh, I imagine she left behind a substantial inheritance," Geneva replied. "Somebody's bound to show up, if only to say thanks."

They knocked at three more houses without learning much more than they knew already. A boy of about eleven, wielding a plastic light saber, said his parents weren't home, but that he had seen an elephant careening through the suburbs earlier that day. He said he and his younger sister had been playing Jumanji and several animals had escaped into the real world, among them an auk, a mountain lion and a giant tarantula.

At the next house over, an old man in a cantaloupe-colored sweater, on hearing that Maribel might have been killed by an exotic animal, laughed until tears streamed from his eyes, then slammed the door so that he could go on laughing.

It was only after they reached the cul-de-sac and circled back around to the other side of the street facing Maribel's house, that their questions began to bear fruit.

"I had to drive the girls to lacrosse earlier," said a woman named Susan with carrot-colored hair. "I came back around four-thirty and there was a woman pulling out of the driveway. I remember being a little taken aback because Maribel almost never has visitors."

"A woman?" said Geneva. "Can you describe her?"

Susan pursed her lips, thinking. "She was youngish-looking, slender, one of those hipster types, with neon pink stripes in her hair and a pair of aviators."

Geneva and Iris exchanged meaningful glances.

"You said she was leaving," said Iris. "How did she leave?"

"She got in her car and drove off. Maribel was sitting on the porch swing, slumped over a little. It looked like she was sleeping. I figured maybe the girl had come by and, seeing that she was asleep, decided it was best not to bother her and left."

This was giving them a better picture of how Maribel had spent her last hours, but it still didn't bring them any closer to knowing the identity of the creature. "You didn't see any animals, though?" Geneva pressed.

"Not so much as an armadillo," said Susan. "I'm so sorry, I wish I could be of more help."

At every door they were given the same answer—no one had seen any suspicious-looking creatures roaming the neighborhood that day. It was beginning to look as though the Wrangler's Devil, in addition to being fierce and deadly, was also a master of stealth and camouflage. It had a near-supernatural ability to slip into a place, make its kill, and then slip out without being seen by anyone in the vicinity.

Which was ridiculous. Geneva grew more and more dubious as the day wore on.

After about an hour of questioning they had managed to interview everyone on the block who had been willing to open their doors. Feeling somewhat defeated, they returned up the street to where Gerry and the lieutenant were examining the boards of the porch for signs of fur or paw prints.

"Well, we learned one thing," said Geneva. "That girl Leora showed up at the house today, but it doesn't sound as though she stayed long. She might have been the last person to see Maribel alive."

"And to think that if she'd only stayed a bit longer," said Gerry, "she might have been able to intervene. Or maybe the creature would have seen them together and figured it was too big of a risk and slunk off."

More than one thing about the case continued to puzzle Geneva. "This supposed critter," she said, "it's usually too afraid of humans to attack them in the middle of the suburbs. Whatever this thing is, it must have been unusually hungry, or else..." She broke off.

"Or else what?" asked Gerry.

"Well, I would like to know just what *sort* of exotic animal we're dealing with—if we're dealing with one at all."

No one had any clue. No real attempt had been made to track the creature, because up to now the stories of disappearing animals had been dismissed as either not vitally important or the fraught imaginings of bored housewives.

"Isn't that typical, though?" said Iris. "No one ever listens to women until they have no other choice."

Gerry said nothing for a moment. He had risen to his feet and was studying his phone with a look of increasing incomprehension.

Geneva was the first to notice that something was wrong. "Gerry, what is it?" she asked. "Are you quite all right?"

Gerry shook his head; his face was an ashen color. "I've just gotten a text from the coroner. She said: 'Forget everything I said earlier. This wasn't the work of an animal, exotic or otherwise. The scratches were made post-mortem to divert suspicion from the real cause of death. Maribel Smythe was murdered by poison.'"

[6]

THE CORONER'S REPORT, Geneva would later tell George, was one of the most disturbing she had heard in all her time as a private investigator. Maribel Smythe had been killed by a heavy concentration of ammonia and bleach, ingested through the nostrils until she passed out. It had taken her upward of half an hour to die. The claw marks had been made by a sharp instrument like a pair of elongated nails in order to create the illusion of death by wild animal.

"We're dealing with a real maniac," said Gerry as they stood in the shade of the porch in the dying light. "Wouldn't be surprised if this person has been stealing and butchering animals across town for the past couple weeks to create the illusion of an exotic animal on the loose as preparation for this murder."

"Who would go through the trouble?" said Iris, aghast.

Geneva said nothing. She was gazing down the street at each house on the block, thinking that each one could be harboring the sort of person who could viciously kill an old woman.

"They did it in broad daylight, too," added Gerry. "I'm telling you, this person is fearless and brazen."

"Or maybe they just snapped," said Geneva quietly.

The two officers and Iris turned to look at her.

"I mean, you saw how she was carrying on last night. She's the sort of person who digs her hooks into a person, fretting and nagging at them until they might explode. We were only sitting together for about twenty-five minutes, but in those few minutes I felt as though I learned... well, all there was to know about her."

Gerry pulled a little steno pad from his front pocket. "You said she was mistreating the waitstaff? I'd like to phone the Swine and find out the name of that man. He might know something."

Geneva was skeptical. "Surely a waiter... I mean, they barely knew each other."

"Remember what we were saying, though," said Iris. "I'd wager she's been to that club before. Although, I figure she's forbidden from returning now."

"I see." Gerry bit off the cap of a pen with his teeth and began to write. "It's entirely possible that after suffering weeks or even months of such mistreatment, a man might track her down to her address and then—" He motioned to the blood-stained floorboards.

Geneva didn't like the direction in which the conversation was trending; it felt as though Gerry had already settled on a suspect and was now seeking reasons to justify it.

"We have to look at the case in terms of personality," she said. "We know that the murderer could be someone sadistic and probably vengeful, and I doubt Maribel could have antagonized a waiter enough to merit that kind of revenge. We're looking for someone well-known to the victim, someone with ample reason to want to hurt her."

It was remarkable how quickly the mood of the discussion shifted once she said this. Gerry lowered his pen. Geneva felt suddenly like she was back in the fifth grade doing the bulk of the work on a group project.

"So," said Gerry, "I guess we need to draw up a list."

"A list, yes," said Geneva. "A list of everyone known to be close to the victim."

But the list wouldn't come until the following day—a day during which it rained in gusts that flooded the sidewalk and bent the slender aspens in the front yard. After lunch, George drove Geneva into town to buy a new raincoat and boots, and on their return home, they lit a candle and sat in the living room for an hour or two playing Scrabble. Geneva won the first two rounds; but seeing that losing repeatedly was putting George in a bad temper, she declined to play her ten-point Q word in the third game, and he won by five. He immediately perked up.

"See, I knew I could do it," he said happily as they rose from the couch where they'd been playing on a coffee table. "Sometimes it just takes me a game or two to get the old gears turning again."

"You did very well," said Geneva. "I wish you could've played against my mom, though. She was an English teacher, too, and in thirty years, I never managed to beat her, not once. She played words I didn't even know existed."

Geneva was now standing in the kitchen scraping raspberry jam over fresh-cut slices of sourdough bread when her phone chimed. Gerry had sent her a single text. *Check your email*, it read.

Geneva brought the plates containing the bread into the living room and set them down on the coffee table in front of

George. "Sit back down, why don't you?" she asked. "Enjoy the snack."

She then ran upstairs and hauled her old laptop back down out of her room and placed it on the kitchen table.

As promised, Gerry had sent her a document containing a short list of names and descriptions.

Janna Olson

Maribel's personal maid / housekeeper. Spoke with her this morning; she seems totally devastated by her employer's death. Has worked in her employ for over two decades. Claims to have been at the supermarket at the time of the murder, though we can't verify this. She made me promise to catch whoever did it.

Dalton Gerard

Maribel's financial advisor. Seen his commercials on TV but still don't know too much about him. Left a message on his voice mail; waiting for him to call back.

Harvey Moore

Maribel's lawn caretaker. He's been in her employ for decades; we spoke over the phone this morning, and I got the sense their relationship was sort of contentious. He sounded drunk, even though it was only ten in the morning. Might want to follow up on this.

J. Jeet Harris

The waiter at the Seven Swine on the night of the altercation. He claims he hadn't encountered the deceased until that night, but I've spoken to multiple people on staff who say she was a regular customer.

Leora Kismet

Presumably a friend of the deceased. You say they were together at the Swine and she was seen pulling out of the driveway just minutes before Maribel was found dead. At present, she's my number one suspect, though I struggle to see what could have motivated her.

One thing I did manage to find out about her: until recently she was married to Hector Kismet, a wealthy big-game hunter who spent much of his twenties and thirties bagging exotic animals in sub-Saharan Africa. He's not a suspect, but I figure *it might be worth paying him a visit, if only to shed some light on Leora's whereabouts (she's been missing since yesterday afternoon, and I haven't been able to get hold of her on her cell.)*

P. S. Apparently my wife knows who Leora is and says she's low-key famous in and around Wrangler's Hill. Why have I never heard of her? I guess I quit listening to new music years ago. But at least it's given me and the missus something to talk about.

Geneva read the suspect list over three or four times, until she felt she had absorbed all the most pertinent facts. She was inclined to rule out the waiter outright, and she felt like including the victim's "lawn caretaker" was a bit of a reach. "Contentious relationship..." Not hard to imagine. "Big-game hunter"—might Mr. Kismet know anything about the wild beast that was rumored to be roaming the streets and corn-fields of Wrangler's Hill? It wouldn't hurt to ask him. Like Gerry, she was inclined to think that questioning Leora would prove their most fruitful course of action; but Leora seemed to have fled shortly after the murder was committed, and that in itself was suspicious.

"Why would she flee," she asked George after sharing the information, "if she had nothing to hide?"

George had brought the bag of grapes and some Brie from the kitchen and was now snatching small bites in between putting the game away. "Could be she didn't know about the murder," he said, "and she's just out of pocket. Remember the time you were trying to get hold of that woman for three days? The lady in charge of the Fun Run?"

"We couldn't get hold of her because she was dead," Geneva reminded him.

"Well, there you go," George replied, with the absolute simplicity of a child. "There could be any number of reasons Leora's away from her phone."

Geneva was still pondering this when her phone chimed again. Thinking it must be Gerry, she reached for it automatically—but the number was unlisted. The text read, *I've got some information that might be of interest to you. The gym at the back of the Bethuel Retreat Center closes at nine tonight. Meet me in the sauna room at a quarter past and bring your friend.*

Geneva dashed off a reply but got no response. She read the message back to George, who murmured and hemmed and hawed and broke off another handful of Brie, looking faintly puzzled.

"You know it's not my place to tell you how to do your job," he said. "But if I was you, I'd be careful."

"*Were* you," said Geneva. "'If I *were* you.'"

George ignored her. "I don't like it," he said. "Someone you've never heard of, who won't tell you their name, asking you meet them at the deserted gym in the middle of the night? I don't like that at all."

Geneva was still reading the text. "How are we even supposed to get into the gym if it's locked?"

"I've been out to Bethuel a couple times. They're not really strict about locking the place down; you're free to come and go as you like. But at least take Iris with you, if you're determined to go."

"I wasn't planning on going alone," said Geneva. "We can go together." She laughed. "And you know, Iris is arming herself these days. We'll be fine."

[7]

Geneva and George and Iris ate a light dinner of eggplant parmesan served with Greek salad and pita bread. George was in a foul mood for some reason, so Geneva was almost glad when he rose, strode over to the hat rack, and announced that he was going to see a William Wordsworth impersonator at the public library.

"He'll be reading excerpts from the *Prelude* and 'Tintern Abbey,'" he said lightly, then resumed that same disgruntled face he had been wearing all night. "Sorry I've been such a sourpuss. Thanks for everything. And you two be careful tonight."

He opened the door and was gone before Geneva could even say bye.

"You watch, he's going to have the time of his life tonight. That impersonator is right up his alley," said Geneva, splitting her bread in half and handing one half to Iris. She thought idly that it looked a bit like a sand dollar that had been broken open.

Iris clucked her tongue. "He hasn't been taking it very well, being bullied by those boys at church. I think it's hitting him particularly hard because they're making him feel weak."

"But that's ridiculous."

Iris nodded. "But when every guy you respect is telling you the same thing," she said, "you start to feel like maybe you're the one with the problem."

Geneva considered this as she ate the last of her bread. She supposed that was why he had been grumpier than usual lately. He was realizing that she and Iris were his only real friends, and George had never been the sort of person to take his true friends for granted. If he seemed a bit over-protective, it was because he realized how precious she was to him and didn't want to lose her—which, given the nature of her work, could happen so easily. The thought made Geneva's heart warm even further toward her teddy-bear of a gentleman friend.

After dinner, the two women passed the time playing Trivial Pursuit, though they didn't "play" so much as read the cards aloud to each other and try to guess the answers. Finally, at about a quarter to nine, Iris said, "You ready to head out?"

They reached Bethuel at about nine. Not having ever been to this particular retreat center, Geneva and Iris made their way to the central building, a spacious, wood-furnished room with benches arranged in rows near the back and a large stone fireplace. Lights hung from rustic, wrought-iron barn chandeliers. The building was empty save for an older gentleman in a forest-brown uniform who was bent low sweeping errant dead leaves into a pile. Around him lay a haphazard pile of dominoes, as if someone playing a game had gotten upset and overturned a table to prevent his competitor from winning.

"Sorry to bother you," said Iris. "Could you point us to the gym?"

The custodian blinked slowly, looking vaguely befuddled. "Don't know what you'd be wanting the gym for. It closed about ten minutes ago."

"We're here to pick someone up," Iris lied.

He blinked again—Geneva was reminded of a sleepy tortoise —and pointed in a northeasterly direction. "Go past the golf course," he said, "past the tennis court and the business office. It'll be on your left."

Thanking him, they both turned and began to leave. Near the door, Geneva stumbled on a full-sized javelin that had been left lying on the rug in front of the fireplace. Its sharp end gleamed in the chandelier lights. Alarmed, she picked it up by the handle and ran back to the custodian.

"Somebody just left this lying on the ground over there," she said. "Imagine if a kid got hold of it."

The custodian accepted the javelin readily, then took it and placed it against the wall next to a rack of pool sticks.

"What would a weapon like that even be doing in a retreat center like this?" asked Geneva as they emerged from the building into the cold night. She was thinking of a movie episode of *Poirot* she had seen in which a woman was killed by a javelin flung across the floor of a gym (a departure from the book, in which the woman had been shot). "Somebody could get really hurt!"

"Sometimes the boys feel like showing off," said Iris. "I remember this place was shut down for a few weeks last summer after a man was killed by a bow and arrow. The killer swore up and down it was an accident, and as no one else was there to witness the killing, they had only his word to go on..."

Following the custodian's directions, they reached the entrance to the gym within a few minutes. Passing through a dimly lit foyer whose blue tiles were damp and black with grime, they entered a room containing a swimming pool six feet deep and about twenty feet wide, with a diving board near the middle that resembled a thin stick of gum.

"If this is closed, I still don't understand why it isn't locked. I'm thinking the sauna must be in here somewhere," said Geneva. As she said this, they heard the patter of wet, bare feet and an old woman wearing a scrub cap emerged from one of the back locker rooms with a towel around her waist. Her short, spiky hair and the way her nose quivered as she passed the two women put Geneva in mind of a hedgehog.

"Don't know what you two are doing here this late at night," she said just as she passed them. "Building's closed."

"We're looking for someone," said Geneva, thinking maybe she could help them.

"Don't know who you could be looking for," she replied, and her nose quivered again. "Ain't no one here."

Finding her slip-on shoes near the front entrance, the woman nodded a curt farewell and left. Now, Iris and Geneva were truly alone in the building, which was silent but for the sound of a distant generator. Outside, the grounds were silent; they and the custodian might have been the only people left on the property. Instinctively, Iris pressed closer to her partner.

"Something very strange about all this," said Iris, as if to justify herself.

Geneva knew what she meant. She had been in empty gyms before, but none like this. The weight of silence was unnerving. Maybe because they were so far out in the country, maybe because George's warning from earlier was continuing to nag at her, maybe because she still couldn't stop thinking of the vicious way the old woman had been attacked and killed only the day before. Somewhere close by, there was a continual drip of water, which reinforced the feeling of being in a cave deep underground.

Nevertheless, they pressed on. Walking in the direction of the lockers from which the hedgehog lady had emerged, they found several empty changing rooms and beyond them a sauna with benches on either side. Steam billowed from the small pool standing in the center of the room amid green tiles, looking like a bowl of ramen newly boiled that was just being served. Geneva and Iris walked in circles around the pool, as if expecting their informant to suddenly spring out of the water.

"It's already twenty past nine," said Geneva. "We probably wasted our time coming out here."

"Well, it's a nice enough night," said Iris, working to put a positive spin on things. "Got us out of the house for a bit. Soon it will be too cold to go anywhere."

But even though to all appearances their informant had stood them up, Geneva still felt an uneasy feeling—an inner conviction that they needed to leave the place as quickly as possible. Every slight noise from the pool room made her flinch. She was beginning to regret that George had made other plans that night, and that he hadn't come with them.

"How long do you think we should wait," she asked, "before we call it a night?"

"Give 'em a few more minutes," said Iris. "We don't know where they're driving from. They might have gotten stuck in traffic."

Geneva shivered, despite the oppressive warmth of the place. "If what they had to tell us was so important, why not just say it over text?"

"More dramatic," said Iris. "They've probably never been an informant before. I bet they find the whole thing very exciting."

Geneva wiped the sweat from her brow with the back of her arm. "Anyway, we can't stay in this sauna much longer. We could get over-heated and—"

Her words were cut short by a noise behind them. Geneva jumped, nearly losing her footing on the slick flooring. At once they both turned to look at the door. It had closed sharply, as if a ghostly wind had nudged it shut. There had been something of a wind that evening, she could recall, but was it enough to actually close a door?

As they both knew, the building was empty. Geneva was not a superstitious person by nature, but the sudden closing of the door badly spooked her. Feeling more certain than ever that they needed to leave, she said, "Few more minutes my foot! We've given this person enough of our time tonight."

Marching back across the room, taking care not to slip on the wet floor, she extended her arm to push the door open again. It wouldn't budge. She tried again with her shoulder, putting the whole weight of her body behind it, but the door did not open. Either it was stuck, or it had been locked or jammed from the outside. Given how rapidly the room was warming, it didn't much matter: they had to get out soon.

With a feeling of growing nervousness, Geneva turned to glance around the room. There were no windows and there would likely be no one to hear them yelling.

"Iris? I believe we're trapped," she said.

[8]

For a moment, Geneva stood motionless, her ear pressed against the door. There were ways out of there. There had to be. Panicking would only fog her mind, the way the steam rising up out of the sauna was now fogging the mirrors lining the walls.

Reaching into her purse, she pulled out her phone and tried to text George, but there was no coverage. Well. That wasn't good.

"What are we going to do?" asked Iris, after a lengthy silence.

"I'm sure someone will be along..." Geneva said boldly even though she had no assurance of such a thing.

"Right," Iris said with a glum look on her face.

Geneva muttered under her breath. Then, walking the perimeter of the room, she began running her hand along the wall tiles on the unlikely chance that maybe there was some secret paneling concealing a passage to another room.

"What are you doing, exactly?" asked Iris, tugging at the damp collar of her dress.

Geneva didn't want to say; she was painfully aware how "Nancy Drew" it would have sounded.

"I don't know," she said. "I don't think there's any way out of here without a window. Why didn't they build windows?"

"Maybe they worried it wouldn't be private enough."

Geneva was barely listening. She calculated that their best hope of escape was banging on the doors and walls, hoping someone passing by might overhear them. How in the world did they get themselves into such a fix? And had someone purposely trapped them? Or had it only been a weird accident? And where in the world was the mystery person who had texted her in the first place?

Without any prior warning to her partner, Geneva strode back over to the door and began slamming her fists against the metal frame. "HELP!" she cried. "IF THERE'S ANYONE OUT THERE, HELP US!"

Following her lead, Iris ran over and began to pound on the door with her. "LET US OUT! PLEASE! IT'S HOTTER THAN THE DEVIL IN HERE!"

They continued to yell like this for some time—in the fog of the moment, Geneva couldn't say how much time elapsed—both of them pounding and calling for assistance until she slumped against the wall, the last of her energy utterly spent.

"Well, if this is how we're going to die," said Iris, wiping the sweat from her neck, "what a way to go."

"You know what's frustrating?" asked Geneva.

"What?"

"We're never going to find out who sent you that text."

"I wish there was a way to trace it," said Iris. She had unbuttoned the two topmost buttons of her blouse. "Maybe after our demise, Gerry will doggedly pursue the killer and avenge us."

This was so unlikely that, in spite of the dire circumstances, they both burst out laughing.

"We had a good run, anyway," said Iris. "Fifteen cases in just under three years—or was it four...? Anyway, there will be a lot of celebrating among the criminal class when we go. They will be pouring champagne."

"If only we could fake our deaths," said Geneva, glad to get her mind off their situation. "Like Poirot did in that one episode. Draw the criminals out of hiding and then bear down on them with righteous wrath."

"Poor Gerry is going to be totally in over his head without us."

"Poor Gerry?" said Geneva. "Poor George!" She pounded on the door again.

They went on like this for a while, exploring the ramifications of their deaths and who would (and wouldn't) be affected by them. They got so lost in speculations that it came as a bit of a shock when they heard what sounded like the scurry of shoes on the tiles outside and the door came open with a sudden jolt.

Geneva had only a moment to reflect that maybe their supposed captor was returning to finish the job when the custodian entered the room, looking slightly dazed.

"What are you two doing in here?" he asked sleepily. "Didn't I tell you that the gym was closed?"

"We were waiting for someone," said Geneva. "We were told to meet him or her here, and they never came."

"Ain't that just the way?" The custodian laughed lightly. He seemed completely unaware of Geneva's and Iris's somewhat frantic state. He stood aside so that they could stagger out.

"Lucky for both of you I was still making my rounds. I s'pose it could have got downright bad in there if I hadn't heard banging and come wandering over to check."

"We're very grateful," said Iris, as she and Geneva emerged into the deliciously cool air of the pool room. Geneva felt as though she had been choking and her lungs had suddenly cleared; she inhaled deep, intoxicating breaths of air.

"And the worst of it is," she told Iris as they returned to the car across the dewy tennis court, "I don't think our anonymous texter even had a single iota of information to share with us."

"Do you think someone trapped us there on purpose?" Iris asked.

"I don't know. And we'll likely never know."

"We are going to report it, aren't we?"

Geneva stood still for a moment. "I'm not convinced it was intentional. I'm not sure I'm ready to report it with so little information."

"But what about the text? And that person never showed. Seems way too fishy to me."

"I suppose you're right," Geneva answered, her mind whirling. Still, at that point, she wanted to keep it on the down low.

"So we've spoken with Maribel's financial manager," said Gerry, when Geneva phoned him the next day to check in. "His name is Dalton Gerard and he's a little sleazy, but he had some very interesting things to tell us."

"Let's hear it," said Geneva.

"Apparently the lady had something like ten different advisors over the years. She kept getting rid of them the second they told her things she didn't want to hear." There was a loud "whoosh-thump!" sound on the other end of the line; it sounded as though Gerry was playing darts in his office. "Anyway, Dalton had been angling for the position for years, and he finally got it shortly before her death."

"Why did he want to be her advisor so badly?"

"I'm getting to that," said Gerry. There was another "thump!" and he swore softly. "He claims it's because he had been a great admirer of Maribel's late father. Naturally, I'm suspicious. So, I do some digging and it turns out her father's financial advisor had been given an enormous gift in the old man's will. Used it to buy three thousand acres of land in Wyoming, that's how big we're talking." Gerry laughed. "Dalton made the mistake of thinking Maribel had inherited her father's generosity."

"Was that everything?"

"Not quite." She waited while he finished re-gathering all the darts or whatever it was he was doing. "Dalton, it transpires, visited Maribel at her home about an hour before the estimated time of death."

Now this was interesting. "Did he give you a precise time?"

"Between three and three-thirty, is what he told me." Geneva could sense that Gerry was building up to his biggest revelation. "Dalton claims Maribel told him she was planning on leaving all her money, her entire fortune, to Janna Olson."

"Her housekeeper?" cried Geneva. "What on earth would possess her do to that?"

"Rich old ladies move in mysterious ways. Maribel must have really loved the lady to keep her in her employ for twenty-some-odd years. By all accounts, she had trouble holding onto anyone for longer than a month or two—if she didn't fire them, they left of their own accord. And this isn't a lady who was known for having friends."

Gerry was doling out so much new information at once that Geneva was having trouble making sense of it all. "But that would seem to suggest, wouldn't it, that Janna had a clear motive for committing the murder?"

"You would think, but in my view, it suggests the opposite," said Gerry. "See, Maribel hadn't actually finished revising her will yet, so far as we know. If Janna had wanted to kill her for money, surely she would have waited." He paused to let this thought linger. "Anyway, we questioned Janna briefly this morning, and I can say with about eighty percent certainty that she knew nothing of Maribel's plans."

This came as a bit of a shock. "She didn't know about the will at all?"

"Not a whiff of it," said Gerry. "When I told her what Dalton told me, she broke down and started crying. Said her employer had been the soul of kindness and she never appreciated her enough while she was living—which I find a little hard to believe, myself."

Geneva shared all this information with Iris over tea when Iris came home from work that night. "So everybody seems to have been expecting money from Maribel, except for Janna who had no idea she was going to be named the sole inheritor?"

Iris tapped at her mug, thinking. "Color me skeptical," she said, "but I'm not so sure Janna has been a perfect angel in all of this, either."

"How do you figure?"

"Don't you remember that old *Twilight Zone* episode, the one about the woman who works as a housekeeper for her mad scientist uncle for twenty-five years, waiting for him to die? And then finally she pushes him down the stairs, and she comes to find out he had built an evil robot that she has to look after, as a condition of inheriting the money?"

Geneva took a sip of her chamomile tea. "I remember it vaguely."

"Well, anyway," said Iris, "what else would motivate a woman to stay for so long in the employ of a rich, miserable, mean old lady? Certainly not love. She must have been expecting some kind of financial compensation."

"Well, there's no harm in hoping, is there?" Geneva replied.

Iris shook her head darkly. "No, but it means we should take her innocent airs and crying jags with a grain of salt. If she tries to tell us she was serving that lady out of the pure goodness of her heart, I'm calling her bluff."

There was a silence in which Geneva finished her tea and set to work eating some of the cheese wedges that were laid out in front of her. As many revelations as they had obtained in the last half-hour, the case remained murky. Geneva still wondered who had lured them to the gym the night before. Though she hadn't reported it and she'd played it down with

Iris, it was still on her mind. Knowing who was behind that could give them an important clue.

Remembering that it had been some time since she had asked about Kayla, Geneva picked up her phone to text Gerry.

Iris, meanwhile, had gotten stuck on *The Twilight Zone.*

"Do you remember the episode where the old man turns out to be an alien prince fleeing his responsibilities by hanging out with a little earth girl? Maybe the killing of Maribel will turn out to be totally justified. Maybe she was secretly an ancient Egyptian queen who had been living for two thousand years and needed to be put down."

Geneva didn't answer; her phone had chimed again, and she was busy reading her latest texts with a look of fixed attention.

"I probably shouldn't have binged the entire third season right before my birthday," said Iris to no one in particular. "Now I keep expecting our murderer to have three eyes, or six arms, or to be six inches tall, or a time-traveler."

"I'm afraid you'll have to get used to more mundane surprises," said Geneva, setting her phone down and beginning to put on her coat. "They've finally located Leora Kismet. She's been hiding out at the home of her ex-husband, Hector. Gerry says she's there now. They've got almost enough evidence on her to make an arrest."

[9]

THE TWO WOMEN made the long drive up to Hector Kismet's house, a sprawling three-story affair with gables and windows sticking out at odd angles and in odd places. It looked as though an architect had designed the place in a manic fit. A dense wood of spruce, poplar and flaming sumac guarded the perimeter of the property, their vibrant colors approaching their zenith in the fullness of fall.

As they neared the house, Geneva was certain she glimpsed a woman's face peering down from behind the curtain of an upstairs window for a split-second. "She's here. You think she'll consent to talk to us?"

"I don't see that she has much choice," replied Iris, bringing the car to a stop along a wall hedged with rhododendrons. "When are the police getting here?"

"Gerry said they were on their way. We've got half an hour to an hour at most before they arrive."

She unbuckled her seatbelt and emerged from the car. No sooner had she done so than a loud noise like a gun blasted above and behind them, terrifying in its suddenness, sending both women scrambling for the protective cover of the front of the car.

"What in goodness's name," said Iris, when the first shock had passed. "Is she shooting at *us*?"

They waited—Geneva felt a terrible agonizing apprehension in the pit of her stomach—but no further shots were fired. Presently, they heard a noise like boots tramping on gravel and a man in an old-fashioned beige uniform, wearing a little round hat like a British colonial officer and carrying a high-powered rifle, strode into view.

"Heartiest apologies," he said, looking more than a little amused by the sight of the crouching, terrified women. "We've all been really jumpy lately, what with the lion or the bear or whatever roaming the neighborhood."

"Does the lion or the bear or whatever drive a car?" Iris replied sardonically.

Hector didn't seem to have heard her. "Anyway, it's not very often that we get visitors out here. Can't say I mind, particularly. An old bachelor like myself could always use the company of a lady."

"We're both taken," said Geneva, still eyeing the rifle with a malevolent glare. "And aren't you married?"

"*Was* married," said Hector, a little sadly. "We were both young and foolish, or, well... she was young, and I was foolish." He laughed unconvincingly. "I'm guessing you're probably here to see her, huh?"

"We would like that," said Geneva. "And could you please dispense with the weapon as soon as humanly possible?"

Hector made no effort to remonstrate. Smiling blandly, he led them to the front of the house and through a pair of immense double doors that put Geneva in mind of a medieval English church. In a cozily furnished sitting room whose heavy brocade curtains obstructed the sunlight, casting a grey pall over the room, Leora was sitting cross-legged on a burgundy pouf, sipping tea from a small china mug. The contrast with her cheery, dim-witted, middle-aged former husband could not have been more striking. There was an intelligence in the girl's slender face, but an intelligence laced with worry and cunning. She had the air of someone who had been ruined by too much thinking.

"I know you two," she said and rose to her feet as they entered. "You'll have to forgive me. I wasn't expecting visitors, or I would have made more tea. Would you like some?"

"Please," said Iris, and Leora bustled off in the direction of what Geneva assumed was the kitchen.

Because Hector insisted on hanging around the sitting room and asking rude questions, Leora invited the two women upstairs to her bedroom. It was surprisingly small considering the size of the house, hardly bigger than a closet, every square inch of wall decorated with posters—Fiona Apple, Florence and the Machine, Aimee Mann, Norah Jones, Regina Spektor.

"I actually got to open for Regina when she rolled through Indianapolis a couple years back," Leora said proudly when they were both seated, Geneva in a rolling desk chair and Iris on the foot of the bed. "Probably the best moment of my professional life. Maybe my whole life."

She spoke in the reserved, unhappy tone of someone who sensed that the best of her life was already behind her, and there was nothing else worth looking forward to.

"I don't want to sugarcoat things," said Geneva. "The police are on their way. It looks very bad for you. You were seen leaving the house just minutes before Maribel's body was found. The two of you had gotten into a spat at the Swine the night before. There are bloody claw marks across the victim's chest, and if I remember correctly, you were wearing long, Wolverine-type nails on your left hand that night."

Leora nodded in resignation, as though she had been expecting this.

"I won't deny that we had our issues," she said. "I wish I could say different. If I could wave a magic wand and change one thing about my life, it would be that." She took a sip of her tea, thinking. "But then, who would I be without her? You get rid of her, you get rid of me."

Geneva grasped the significance of this statement about a second before Iris, who whispered in a tone of surprise, "She was your *mother*."

Tears darted into Leora's eyes and she turned her head, looking a little embarrassed.

"But I've done some preliminary research," said Geneva, "and it doesn't seem you were raised by her."

"She didn't raise me," Leora managed to say. "I guess I should say, she raised me until the age of six. Then I was... well, rescued by someone. I was put into a foster home, then adopted and given to a good family. I should have hated Maribel, should have wanted her dead for some of the things she had done to me. And I won't pretend those feelings didn't resurface, from time to time. But when you're little, your love for your parents is unconditional. You want more than anything to be loved by them. I've spent the bulk of my life trying to earn her love. The second I was old enough, I went looking for her."

This was a frank and surprising confession, but Geneva could sense there was much she had left out. "I know this can be hard to talk about," she said, "so you don't have to tell me. But I would like to know what she did to you."

Leora didn't answer. Her eyes had drifted to a *Phantom of the Opera* poster thumb-tacked just above the headboard of her bed.

Iris, meanwhile, was studiously examining a tiny ornate magenta box that was lying half-hidden beneath a duvet, as if Leora had hastily flung the duvet over it when she saw them pulling into the drive.

"Is that a jewelry box?" asked Iris. "It's really lovely."

Leora shook her head with a pained expression. "It's stupid, really. It's my lyric box. My old boyfriend gave it to me when I was sixteen. One of the nicest presents I've ever gotten. He was killed in an accident coming home from a football game one Friday night and this little souvenir is all I have of him. I've held onto it."

Iris knelt and picked it up, cupping it in her hands like a small turtle. "Do you mind if I look at it?" she asked, and with her customary lack of propriety, she had already opened it before Leora could say otherwise. Iris scanned the lyrics scrawled in glittery purple pen by a teenaged hand. Her mouth narrowed into a thin line, and her face assumed a troubled expression.

She glanced up at Leora, who was busily fidgeting with a paperweight on her desk. "You were really angry, weren't you?"

"I was sixteen," said Leora. "Who doesn't resent their parent at sixteen?"

"This is beyond resentment, though," said Iris. "You talk about wanting to brick her up in a cellar and drink champagne as you savor her dying screams."

"We had just finished reading 'The Cask of Amantillado' in AP English," Leora replied. "I thought referencing Poe would be goth and edgy."

"And what's all this about being born in prison, unaware of the existence of a world outside—"

With a sudden swooping movement, like a vulture descending, Leora reached down and snatched the box up out of Iris's hand. "Whatever you're looking for," she said, "you're not going to find it in there."

"Did you kill your mother?" asked Geneva, who had been watching her intently the whole time.

Leora was silent.

Ignoring her sullen gaze, Geneva pressed. "What were you doing over at the house?"

"She invited me over, and we got into a tiff. It's getting to the time of year when her moods were particularly bad. She hated autumn and the whole holiday season—I think because everyone's attention was on the holidays and not her. We exchanged some words and I stormed off."

"What did you fight about?" asked Iris.

Leora shrugged as if to say, "Does it really matter?"

"We're not trying to pry into your personal life," said Geneva. "We would like to help you."

"Well, you've already basically told me you think I killed my own mother," said Leora. "So thanks, but no."

"We never said we thought you killed her." Geneva leaned forward as if to lay a hand on her arm but refrained. "The fact that all the evidence is pointing in your direction makes me wonder. We could be dealing with a terrifyingly clever killer."

"Or maybe I snapped and did something that I'll regret for the rest of my life."

"Where did you go after leaving your mother's house?"

"I was feeling pretty angry, so I just drove." Leora flung herself onto the bed and grabbed a little stuffed pig, hugging it to her chest as if wanting the interview to be over. "I didn't really know or care where I was going."

"Did you stop anywhere?"

Leora shook her head. "No... wait, yes. I stopped at a gas station to fill up the car and buy one of those sixty-four-ounce sodas. They were on special."

Geneva made a mental note to check that. Outside, the sun was slowly setting, casting a golden hue over the sleepy bedroom. It was around the time of day when George normally came over, kicked off his shoes near the door and took a nap on the sofa. Geneva didn't often think of him when she was working, but just now she found herself missing him acutely.

She figured Leora must hate them for coming, so it came as a surprise when she said quietly, "You don't have to leave just yet. Maybe it's better to have someone with me when the police come."

"Have you ever been to jail before?" asked Iris, more in sympathy than curiosity.

"No, never. Been suspended from school a few times."

"Haven't we all," Iris replied.

Just then there was a low tap at the door. Geneva sat up straighter in her chair. She couldn't remember hearing any footsteps in the corridor; she wondered if Hector had been listening to them this whole time.

"You can come in," said Leora in an unwelcoming tone.

Hector stuck his broad head in, bronze curls spilling out from beneath his ridiculous hat. "I don't mean to interrupt," he said, "but when are the police getting here?"

It was at this moment that Geneva's phone chimed. She reached for it mechanically but with an odd feeling of foreboding that was confirmed seconds later as she read the text.

"They're not coming," she said in a tone of faint surprise. "Harvey Moore, the gardener, has just been arrested and is being driven to the station. The police raided his home and searched his computer; apparently they have ample proof that he had been planning to poison Maribel."

[10]

Within the next couple hours, Geneva and Iris had left Leora and made their way to the station, where they were debriefed by Gerry on the events leading up to Harvey's arrest. Based on the man's website searches, it was clear he had been hoping to poison Maribel using widely available lawn chemicals which he had purchased the weekend before at the local home improvement center.

"Over the years, Maribel's gardener has purchased vast amounts of lawn care equipment specifically for Maribel's property," said Gerry. "He seems to have been getting frustrated that he was putting all this work into someone's lawn and wasn't even getting paid decent wages for it. And I mean, who could blame him?"

"I don't like to speak ill of the dead," said Iris, who had spoken ill of the dead many times, "but I get the impression this woman cheated everyone whoever worked for her."

"You're not wrong," said Gerry, his gaze drifting ruefully to a framed portrait of Kayla that he kept on his desk. She was eating a chocolate-chip cookie the size of her face, the sun setting over the blood-tinged sea behind her. "What clinches it, in my opinion, is that Harvey set up his own business almost the second after Maribel's death."

"His own business?" said Geneva. "Didn't he already have one?"

Gerry shook his head with an air of distraction. "One of the stipulations of his contract with Maribel is that he would work for her exclusively, which precluded him from adopting any new clients. Of course, Harvey only agreed to this condition under the presumption that she would pay him the wages he was owed, which she did not."

Geneva was sitting opposite Gerry with her hands steepled. "But of course, the fact that he had incentive to kill her doesn't mean that he did it. Pretty much everyone had incentive to kill her."

"Perhaps," said Gerry. "But in this instance the facts seem pretty damning."

They were shown into a familiar room at the back of the station where Harvey was seated anxiously twisting his hands as he sipped coffee from a white Styrofoam cup. His hands were gnarled and knotted like an old oak, as if he had been tending lawns for a hundred years instead of just twenty.

"I'll be honest with you," he told them, "I never liked the woman. Right hand to God, I felt a wave of relief when I found out she had kicked it."

"Your complete lack of remorse isn't doing you any favors, Mr. Moore," said Geneva.

"Can you look me in the face and tell me you're upset that she's dead?" Harvey replied.

Geneva ducked the question by quoting some lines from Donne. "'Any man's death diminishes me, because I am involved in mankind.'"

"She was a Scrooge. The world is a merrier place tonight because of her death."

Harvey hadn't yet grasped that Iris and Geneva were listening intently. With each incriminating statement, his grave seemed to widen.

"It might help if you could tell us where you were on the afternoon of her death," said Iris. "When was the last time you saw her alive?"

"Based on the estimated time of death," said Harvey, "about half an hour before she died."

He smiled a little ghoulishly at the effect of this statement on the two women.

Geneva said nothing for a moment. She was thinking furiously. If Dalton had been to the house only an hour before the murder, and Harvey had dropped by a half-hour later... what did it mean? She sensed she was close to an answer, but for the moment it continued to elude her.

"Did you speak to her?" she said aloud.

Harvey shook his head. "No, I didn't get a chance to. I knocked at the door, but I don't think she heard me. There was too much else going on. Too much noise."

This was interesting. "What sort of noise?"

"A nasty argument, it sounded like. Between her and one other person. The second female would try to speak and would be drowned out by Maribel's voice. Figuring it would be best if I came back at a later time, I turned to leave. But right as I was crossing the lawn, I heard Maribel say, very loudly, 'YOU CAN FORGET IT. YOU'RE NOT GETTING A SINGLE PENNY FROM ME.'"

Geneva glanced crosswise at Iris. Leora had mentioned earlier that she and her mother had had an ugly spat shortly before the body was discovered, though she declined to say what they had argued about. Now it appeared that mystery had been solved, at least.

"Where did you go after you left the house?" Geneva asked.

"I drove straight home."

"Can anyone verify that?"

"The lousy driver I flipped off in traffic."

Harvey's dismissive tone was beginning to grate on her nerves. "Mr. Moore, I don't know if you realize the amount of trouble you're potentially in. There's evidence you were planning to poison the woman. You're known to have bought poison last weekend. You didn't even wait until her body was cold before filing to start your own business. Based on the police report, it appears you needed her dead so that you could steal her extensive list of rich contacts."

Harvey shrugged, as if to say that was all more or less correct. "I'll say this," he said, still twisting his knotted hands. "I was as surprised as anyone when the old bat joined the invisible choirs. I didn't want to be the one to kill her, you understand? I just wanted her dead. I prayed to God that I wouldn't have to get my hands dirty—and lo and behold, sometimes it seems God really does answer our prayers."

They emerged from the station into a cool, tranquil gloom. It was past nine and a gusty wind shivered the rows of corn in the fields that hedged the highway and made the sumacs tremble.

"They can't both have done it," said Geneva. "Can they?"

"How do you figure?" asked Iris.

"I mean there's abundant evidence incriminating both Leora and Harvey. She has a motive now, if she didn't have one before. Maribel had invited her to the house that afternoon and informed her that she was cutting her entirely out of the will. The fact that Leora failed to mention this when we interviewed her isn't helping her case."

Iris slowed to allow an eighteen-wheeler to pass. "How many people dropped by the house that day? It's getting more crowded than Times Square on New Year's Eve."

"Three that we know of," said Geneva, who had been busily organizing the chronology of events in her head. "She met with her financial advisor about an hour before her death and informed him that she was planning on leaving all of her money to Janna. Then shortly after Dalton left, Leora dropped by and they had a fight in which Maribel announced that she was disinheriting her. That altercation was overheard by Harvey, who had shown up to ask her a question, about half an hour before she died."

Iris clucked her tongue. "It certainly doesn't look good for Leora, does it?"

Geneva had to admit that it didn't. She took out her phone, which she had placed on silent at the station, and began to read through her new messages. There was one from George wanting to know when they were coming home—he suffered from seasonal depression and got particularly lonely during the fall months—and another from a number she didn't recognize.

Just a tip from a friend, read the text. *Please don't reply to this message. I attend Sacred Communion Catholic Church with Janna Olson and I've noticed that she's been going to confession seemingly every day for the past week. For the past four or five days she's been at mass every time the doors open, which if you know Janna, is not like her.*

Geneva read the message to Iris, who pursed her lips and made a sudden, sharp U-turn.

"Wait, where are we going?" Geneva exclaimed. "We were nearly home."

"Didn't Maribel and Janna live together? Or if not exactly live together, didn't Janna spend a whole lot of time there?" asked Iris, accelerating to sixty. "I think it's about time we paid her a visit."

Janna, however, wasn't at Maribel's home.

"Seems a waste to have driven all the way here," said Geneva, gazing forlornly up the drive as they sat in their parked car. "You think maybe she left the door unlocked?"

"Normally I wouldn't advise entering someone's home without their consent or knowledge," said Iris, already removing the keys from the ignition. "But I mean, why not? I figure we can beg forgiveness from Gerry later."

They crept up the drive toward the porch where Maribel's body had been found. Geneva was wishing she had worn darker clothing rather than the eggshell-white cardigan and white floral-patterned skirt she was wearing. She tapped at the door just to make doubly sure no one was inside, then attempted to force the handle. It wouldn't yield.

Resigned to defeat, they were making their way back to the car when Geneva's attention was drawn to an object lying beneath the green trash bin at the front of the drive. It looked as though it had fallen from the top of the garbage pile when the house had been cleaned. Telling Iris to wait by the car, she ran to fetch it.

It was a pillow, or it had once been a pillow, embroidered with some sort of forest scene. It appeared to have been inelegantly ripped into pieces by a determined hand, straight down the middle, and bits of cotton stuffing were falling out and being scattered by the wind across the damp street and the wet, rainy lawn. More curiously still, it looked as though someone had recently attempted to sew the pillow back together before giving up after only a few stitches.

"What's going on there?" said Iris, when Geneva returned to the car carrying what remained of the battered pillow. "Did this pillow hurt someone and they decided to get revenge?"

Geneva, meanwhile, was already texting Gerry. "Maybe he knows where she is at this hour. If not, he could at least give us her number. After seeing this, I think it's imperative that we talk to her."

"I don't get it, though," said Iris. "Why go out of your way to eviscerate a pillow?"

Gerry had no idea where Janna had gone or where she was. He did confirm, however, that Janna stayed over at Maribel's often. But he warned Geneva not to go mucking about that night. "Listen, I want you to head straight home and lock your doors. There's been another animal killing, and it's grisly."

At present, however, Geneva wasn't interested in new killings, animal or otherwise. "Please, I just need to know how we can contact Janna."

Gerry forwarded her Janna's number, but reiterated his warning that they go home. "And tell that boyfriend of yours to stay home, too. You wouldn't believe what I've seen in the past hour."

Ignoring his warning, Geneva texted Janna, who wrote back in less than a minute. "She says she's up for a chat, if we are."

"So where are we headed?" asked Iris, bringing the car to a start.

"Back to Bethuel," Geneva replied. "The gym's just closed and she's hanging out in the lounge by herself."

[11]

First, however, they dropped by the house to pick up Iris's police scanner so that they could hear the news flowing in about the latest killing. They plugged it into the charger in Iris's car. It seemed a woman living on Quincy at the outskirts of town had entered her chicken coop at about a quarter past seven to find a nightmarish tableau—the entire coop splattered with blood and animal entrails, feathers drifting here and there like the first snow of winter.

With a feeling of morbid curiosity, Geneva entered the woman's address into the GPS and drew in a sharp intake of breath. "Iris," she exclaimed, "that's about half a mile from where we're headed!"

"And yet somehow I keep driving," said Iris. "What is wrong with us? And why in the world am I driving so quickly right back to the place where we were recently spooked within an inch of our lives?"

"You're right," Geneva said, not exactly excited about returning to the retreat center where the sauna was either. But they needed to talk to Janna.

They reached the retreat center about a quarter to ten. As before, the grounds were virtually empty; the custodian who had let them out on their previous visit waved curtly from the window of an office he was vacuuming as they ran past. They found Janna seated alone at a long bench in the dining hall, clutching her rosary beads and praying fervently.

"Janna, I don't mean to interrupt," said Geneva, "but we need to make this quick-like. There's a... a *creature* loose, and it's hungry tonight. The police are urging everyone to head home and lock their doors."

Janna didn't respond. Geneva stepped forward, prepared to grab her by the hand and lead her back to her car if she had to —but then she saw the tears streaking her face, the look of utter despair and remorse in her eyes, and she guessed all.

"Recently, I developed rheumatism," Janna said, slowly and quietly. "I've been in the most unbearable pain, and I thought Maribel would understand, but she didn't. She could be a hard, hard woman. But foolishly, I believed I was more than her employee. I considered myself her friend. Turns out, that didn't go both ways. She continued to chastise me for not doing my work properly. I just got fed up... hadn't I served her faithfully all these years, and then, for her to treat me like that...? It was getting to be too much." She looked at them with teary eyes. "A woman can only take so much." She clucked her tongue as if commiserating with herself.

Geneva bent close. Her voice was soft. "Is that what pushed you over the edge?"

"Not quite." Janna clutched her frail hands miserably. "Twenty years ago, I did something behind Maribel's back that she never knew about. Never, never, not for all these years. Until last week."

Her voice caught and she took in a shaky breath before continuing, "Maribel had raised poor Leora basically as a prisoner. She kept her locked up in her bedroom until the age of six and had her convinced that their home was the only building in existence, and that we were the only people in it. I called the Child Protective Services and told them everything. They took Leora away and put her in foster care, where she was eventually adopted by a loving family."

Geneva was beginning to understand now. "The conversation..." she said slowly. "The one that Harvey overheard from the front porch... she wasn't talking to Leora, she was talking to you. She was cutting you out of her will for betraying her."

Janna nodded with difficulty. "She had been planning to reward me for all my years of service. Which, as you can guess, came as a complete surprise to me. But then, when she confronted Leora that afternoon and informed her that she was taking her out of the will, Leora decided to hurt her in the most painful way she knew how—by admitting the truth we had been keeping secret her whole life."

Janna wiped at her tears. "Why Leora would do that, I just don't understand. But it worked. Maribel was outraged. She summoned me into her room and informed me that she had changed her mind after all. In the space of about an hour, between Dalton's visit and Harvey's, I lost everything."

"What did you do?" Iris asked and then knowing dawned on her, too. "How did you do it?"

Janna looked pained by the question. "I don't know what came over me. At first, I was only going to berate her verbally... but I guess the weight of all those years of abuse finally caught up to me and something broke. Something inside me just went crazy. It wasn't even about the money. It *wasn't*."

She inhaled deeply and dropped her rosary in her lap. "I-I went crazy. I made a mixture of ammonia and bleach and poured it into a bucket. I knew it was deadly. I-I threw a towel over Maribel's head and stuck the bucket in her lap. I was like a beast. I became physically stronger than I really am. I was so... so *angry*. Before she could fight me off, she sucked in enough breaths to, to..."

Janna went quiet and a faraway look filled her eyes. "I still can't believe how strong I became ... even with this rheumatism. I would have never believed it. Given how old Maribel was, she succumbed quite quickly. I was horrified, of course. I felt like I was stumbling through a nightmare. I-I didn't know what to do. So I cleaned up everything and left."

Geneva studied the old woman with a look of shock mingled with sympathy. "Did you carve the claw marks into her chest and neck?"

Janna shook her head. "No." Her voice was dull. "It was Leora who did that."

Both Iris and Geneva were taken aback. "Leora?"

"She's spent years thinking she owed me for saving her life. She's been looking for a way to repay me. But I guess... I guess something in her snapped, too, when she betrayed me to Maribel. Later, she felt horrible about the whole thing. All of it. Even felt bad about upsetting Maribel. Not that long after she'd left the first time, she drove back to the house to apologize."

Janna inhaled sharply. "She found Maribel slumped dead on the front porch. She called me first to tell me about Maribel being dead, and by my voice, she knew something bad had happened. I-I tried to lie to her. But she guessed. She guessed everything except the mixture of ammonia and bleach. She felt responsible somehow. She wanted to help me, so she dug the long nails she wears onstage out of her purse and used them to deface the body just enough that the police would see the marks and think that animal running around had done it. She was hoping to divert all suspicion away from me. She figured she owed me that much."

Janna shrugged her bony shoulders. Sorrow emanated from her like a rolling wave.

"And the pillow?" said Iris. "The one that you must have sliced to bits?"

"I-I... I was stricken with guilt," said Janna. "I had to take it out on something. I regretted it almost immediately. In a few minutes none of this will matter, though." She removed a crystalline vial from her handbag. "I've said my last prayers. I have no intention of going to prison—I'd never survive it. Never. I pray God will forgive me for this..."

Geneva gazed in disbelief at the vial of poison, trying to calculate whether she could reach it in time to wrest it out of Janna's hands.

"Stop. Please. You don't have to go this way," she said. "I understand that you're suffering, I know your guilt must be great—"

Iris grabbed Geneva's arm, spluttering in incoherent terror which, Geneva felt, was slightly out of proportion to the situation. Attempting to maintain a level calm, she said, "Before you do anything rash, let's talk about this, please."

But Janna never responded, for it was at this moment that Iris pointed through the open door to the back terrace behind the gym and shouted, "LOOK!"

What Geneva saw there was enough to drive all thoughts of murder and poison completely from her mind.

Slowly stalking across the patio, its silver-grey fur damp and gleaming in the porch light, was an immense leopard, gazing directly at the three women with eyes that burned golden one moment, green the next. It emitted a noise that was half-purr, half-growl, flexing its long claws and clicking them effortlessly on the cement like a Spanish bull preparing to charge.

"Well," said Iris in a low voice, "I think now we know what's been killing Gladys's chickens."

Geneva hesitated, rooted to the spot, not knowing whether to remain still or to run. Fresh tears poured from Janna's face as she grabbed her rosary beads and began reciting the Our Father in an impassioned voice.

"That thing is about to pounce on us," said Geneva. "Can I make it to the door in time to shut it?"

"Not unless you want to be its next meal," said Iris.

But given their present locations, it was evident that Janna, as the nearest one to the door, would be the first to go.

"Janna," said Geneva. "I need you to get over here, *now*."

Janna said nothing, so absorbed in her prayers that she didn't seem to have heard her.

"JANNA!"

Geneva yelled it so loudly that Janna rose and began stumbling in the direction of the two women without remonstration.

The three of them stood together, arms linked, each certain now that death was imminent. The leopard continued to slink forward, crossing the patio in slow strides and entering the room, its bewhiskered face in the midst of those long, low benches, the pool table, and the rustic chandeliers looking horrible and surreal.

"It's already eaten tonight," said Iris. "It ate something like ten chickens, so if we just—"

"Iris, *please*," said Geneva sharply. "For once I need you to just be quiet."

Iris fell obediently silent. The leopard raised its head, sniffed, and gazed malevolently at the women with a look that left

Geneva in no doubt but that it intended to kill them. Then, opening its broad mouth to reveal its rows of freshly stained teeth, it let out a growl that seemed to sap all the remaining strength from her body.

With a faint feeling, Geneva reached for Iris's hand. "I suppose we always knew this is how it was going to end," she said quietly. "The two of us standing side by side."

Iris didn't say a word this time, only took her hand in hers and squeezed it tightly.

The leopard crouched low and prepared to spring.

It was at this moment, however, that hope arrived from an unlikely source. Entering the room from the back door nearest the kitchens, Officer Sheehan surveyed the scene at a glance. Then, reaching for the belt at his waist, he retrieved his gun and motioned for the women to get behind him.

"Y'all cover your ears," he said.

He leveled the gun and fired. Nothing but an empty click.

He fired again. Still nothing.

Sheehan swore under his breath. The leopard was about six feet away now. Sensing an opportunity, it took a soaring leap through the air—

... and landed with a thud on the floor just inches from where Geneva was standing, a javelin rammed through its heart.

Gasping in mingled terror and relief, the women turned to see the face of their rescuer and found Gerry standing over by the rack containing the pool sticks, smiling a good-natured smile.

"Gerry, I can't believe it!" cried Iris, running over and throwing her arms around him and kissing him twice on the cheeks for good measure. "If you hadn't... I mean if you..."

And here, Iris broke down sobbing, for once in her life at a complete loss for words.

[12]

Badly shaken by her brush with death, Janna yielded herself to the police that night and made a full confession. When Geneva next spoke with her a few days later, she seemed at peace with herself even though she was petrified about prison.

"But I have to pay for my crimes," she said quietly. "I sinned in a moment of weakness, and I've got to atone for it. Such is the way of things."

"Such is the way of things," Geneva murmured after her.

"So odd having that javelin there in the first place," Janna said.

But Geneva remembered gratefully when Iris had handed it to the janitor who had then carelessly left it right there by the pool sticks.

Relief rippled through Wrangler's Hill as news of the leopard's demise made its way through the community. Turned out the leopard was being kept illegally by a bloke outside of town. The animal had escaped, and of course, it wasn't reported—couldn't have been reported—since the animal wasn't legal in the first place. The owner had been desperately trying to re-capture it, but his efforts had been in vain. There was now hope that the smugglers who had brought the animal into the country would be caught.

Gerry, used to being dismissed by his older colleagues, suddenly found himself in the unlikely position of media darling. For most of the next week he was out of the office, recounting the killing on local morning shows and public radio—a story which grew in the telling, and now involved him wrestling the leopard to the ground with a sassy quip while the women wept in dismay.

Yet none of the media attention pleased him half so much as his wife's. On a cold, breezy night in late September, Kayla invited him out to Sandy Point, where they cried and held hands, and she apologized for having been so distant of late.

"I don't know what came over me," she said. "I suppose at my age I just needed a break. But I'm over it now, and I'm ready to go on being your loving wife."

And throwing her arms around him, she kissed him until her lips were sore.

Near the end of that week came another surprising bit of news: Harvey Moore was arrested for luring Geneva and Iris to the retreat center with mal intent. Iris had ended up blathering on about their scare over dinner one night, which had alarmed George to such an extent that he'd taken it straight to Gerry.

The police had traced the anonymous text directing them to the sauna room back to the source, and found it belonged to a burner phone Harvey had purchased from a vendor at the farmer's market. Detained at the station, Harvey admitted that he feared the two women were going to link him to the crime despite him having not committed it. He'd wanted to scare them away from the investigation or, as he delicately put it, "get them out of the way" before they did any further harm.

"The irony of it all," said Gerry as he recounted this to the two women, "is he could have avoided prison if only he hadn't panicked. As it is, he's looking at being sentenced for his own stupidity."

"He would have killed Maribel too, given another week or two," said Geneva. "It was only the timely intervention of Janna that spared him in the first place."

"It just goes to show, you shouldn't go around planning murders," said Gerry, pulling a dart from where it rested above his ear like a pencil. He tossed it at the board where it landed with a perfect bull's eye. "One of these days, the law is always gonna catch up with you."

On the first weekend of November, a weekend that was overcast and intermittently drizzling, Gerry and Kayla and Geneva and George along with Iris went out dancing at the local dance center. It was Discount Dance Night and tickets were seven dollars at the door. George wore his finest charcoal gray suit—slightly worn, with fraying patches at the elbows—while Geneva wore a flowing green silken dress the precise color of a peacock's tail, with a feather in her hair to match.

Much to her surprise, everyone on the dance floor turned and applauded as the five of them entered the room together. In hardly more than a moment the assembled dancers were pumping their fists and chanting in unison, "Gerry! Gerry! Gerry!"

Gerry, who by this point was getting heartily sick of the adulation, merely raised one hand into a fist and smiled a wan smile.

"Well, I don't know about you guys," said Iris, giving Geneva a curt pat on the arm and beginning to wade out onto the floor, "but it's been a long week, and I think I've earned the right to put on some moves!"

Just as she said this, a hip-hop song began to play. With a look of pure joy, Iris spread her arms wide and moved her hips in time with the bassoons. Geneva exchanged glances with George, and both of them suppressed a laugh.

With a chaste kiss on the lips, Kayla took Gerry by the hands and pulled him onto the floor. George offered Geneva his arm and together the two stepped forward together, looking like a couple of picnic-goers walking along a sunny beach.

"Do you think we'll ever have a solid two weeks where nothing happens?" she asked. "Just an interrupted fortnight of lazing about not having to worry about killers and thieves and escaped leopards?"

"I doubt it," said George. "After about half a day, you'd get depressed and go looking for a crime to solve."

Geneva supposed this was probably true. Just then a swift elbow nudged George and one of his church friends, a gentleman in his forties with close-cropped hair and ears that were big and scaly like an armadillo, tried to move him rudely aside. "Give someone else a turn with the lady, will you?" he said over the wail of the synths. "She might be surprised to learn there are other men out there."

"Other men? Yes," said Geneva. "Other men worth dating? I doubt it."

And, to the surprise of both men, she grabbed George by the arm and pulled him close, and together they danced through the rainy and raucous night.

The End

CONTINUE READING...

Thank you for reading *Poison & Porches!* **Are you wondering what to read next?** Why not read *Fashion & Fatality?* **Here's a sneak peek for you:**

It was the first week of March and for the first time in nearly six months, it was warm enough to go out riding. Sensing that this reprieve in the weather might not last, Harry Nichols and his brother Paul had taken their four-wheelers and were now riding them up and down the streets of their Indiana neighborhood—which was just outside the city limits. Of course, they knew they shouldn't be riding them on the public roads, but the temptation was simply too great.

"Hang on, I want to see how fast I can take this thing!" Harry shouted as they turned in the cul-de-sac, only narrowly avoiding a mailbox with a wooden scarecrow peeking over its edge. Normally their mother would have warned them against attempting to go at full speed, but she had been all but absent from the house lately, trapped in committee meetings until nearly midnight and only giving them a cursory "good night" as she came through the door on the way to her bedroom.

"Don't go too fast, now," said Paul. "Remember the time you almost wrecked the Morrigans' Hummer because you wasn't watching where you was goin'?"

"Oh, come off it!" cried Harry. "You're beginning to sound just like Mom and Richard." Although Richard was their biological father, they had always addressed him by his first name. Harry couldn't even remember why, now. Probably because it irritated him.

Bringing the speed up to sixty-five, Harry loosened his grip on the steering wheel and slowly rose in his seat until he was standing almost at full height. The feel of the wind on his face was exhilarating. He wished the street could have stretched on forever so he wouldn't have to worry about slowing to a halt at the next stop sign in approximately four seconds. Next weekend, he was heading down to his cousin Luke's—*sans* Paul—who owned a farm with a dirt road that went on for mile after mile. They'd eat whatever they wanted, play Halo and stay up drinking in the barn until all hours.

He made a U-turn at the corner and sped back past their house just as his brother drove past him headed in the other direction. It was only as he approached the cul-de-sac for the second time that the real trouble started—which Harry would have noticed if he had been going just a bit slower and paying more attention.

Harry didn't know much about the couple that lived next door. The old lady dressed in fancy clothes and ran some kind of high-end clothing store in downtown Wrangler's Hill. Harry didn't mind her so much. It was her husband.

Click Here to Continue Reading!

http://ticahousepublishing.com/cozy-mystery.html

Donna Muse has been a mystery buff for years! But she hasn't been a fan of blood and gore. So when the Cozy Mystery genre came into being, she jumped on board with both feet. She loves the amateur sleuth and is fascinated by the intense and often comical way the perpetrator is revealed. Donna lives in Maine with her husband, loves walking by the surf, fishing for striped bass, and playing with her grandchildren and her cats.

contact@ticahousepublishing.com